This
David Bennett Book
belongs to

_____

_____

_____

_____

_____

For my friend Kulwinder, her husband Rajinder,
their son Aranjeet and his baby sister Jasmine
with love,
Jackie.

First published in Hardback in 2000
by David Bennett Books Limited, United Kingdom.
This Paperback edition published 2000.
Text copyright © 2000 David Bennett Books Limited.
Illustrations copyright © 2000 Jacqueline McQuade.
Style and design of all titles in the Teddy Bear series
copyright © 1995 David Bennett Books Limited.
Jacqueline McQuade asserts her moral right to be
identified as the illustrator of this work.

ISBN 1 85602 398 2
Manufactured in China

A Baby Sister for Teddy Bear

Jacqueline McQuade

DAVID BENNETT BOOKS

Teddy's Mum is going to have a baby. Mum puts Teddy's paw on her tummy so Teddy can feel the baby making little kicks!

Teddy and Dad are busy in baby's room making sure that everything is ready. Babies need lots and lots of things!

Grandma and Grandpa come to take care of Teddy. Teddy gives Mum a big hug before she goes to the hospital with Dad.

"Soon you'll be a big brother," Grandpa tells Teddy. They all wonder if the new baby will be a boy or a girl.

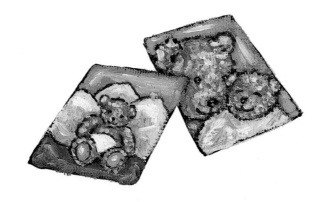

It's a girl! Grandma and Grandpa take Teddy to the hospital to meet his baby sister for the very first time. He is so excited!

At home, Grandpa and Grandma give presents to Teddy and the baby. Teddy's present says, 'For a best-ever brother'.

Teddy's baby sister drinks milk from her bottle and afterwards goes 'burp'. "Isn't she funny?" laughs Teddy.

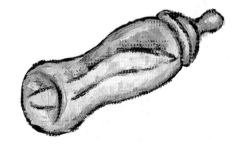

Lots of friends come to Teddy's house to see the new baby. Teddy tells them all about being a big brother.

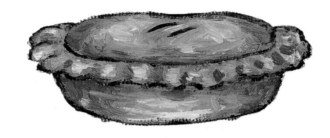

Dad and Teddy take baby out for a walk. "This was your pram when you were a tiny baby," says Dad.

Baby's bathtime is fun!
While Mum washes baby,
Teddy shows her his
favourite squeaky duck.
She smiles and gurgles!

Teddy giggles as Mum sprinkles baby's clean bottom with talcum powder. She puts baby into a fresh, soft nappy.

It's time to say goodnight.
Mum gives Teddy a big hug
and tucks him into bed.
"You're still my favourite
baby boy," she says.